P9-CQW-827

First published in Japan in 1981 by Child Honsha Co., Ltd. under the title *Nezumi no Sakanatsuri*.
First published in the United States, Great Britain, Canada, Australia, and New Zealand in 2011
by North-South Books Inc., an imprint of NordSüd Verlag AG, CH-8005 Zürich, Switzerland.
Translated by Missy Debs. Edited by Susan Pearson.
Distributed in the United States by North-South Books Inc., New York 10017.
Library of Congress Cataloging-in-Publication Data is available.
Printed in Germany by Grafisches Centrum Cuno GmbH & Co. KG, 39240 Calbe, June 2011.
ISBN: 978-0-7358-4048-5 (trade edition)
1 3 5 7 9 • 10 8 6 4 2

www.northsouth.com

FSC
www.fsc.org
MIX
Paper from
responsible sources
FSC® C043106

Seven Little Mice
Have Fun on the Ice

by **Haruo Yamashita**

illustrated by
Kazuo Iwamura

NorthSouth
New York / London

This is the story of seven little mice. They are septuplets, which is like twins only there are seven.

It was winter, but the seven little mice didn't mind the cold. "We're going skating on the lake!" they announced when they got home from school.

The seven little mice loved to skate.

"Let's go to the middle of the lake!" "Last one there's a rotten egg!" "Who's holding my tail?" "Uh-oh!"

CLANG! CLANG! What was that noise?

Little Weasel and his father were making a hole in the ice.

What were they going to do?

Little Weasel dropped his line into the hole and started to fish.

"Come here, little fish!" said Father Weasel.

No sooner had he spoken than silver fish started to tug on Little Weasel's line.

"Look at all the fish I caught!" shouted Little Weasel. He was very proud.

"Let's go ice fishing tomorrow!" begged the seven little mice that evening.

"I can't tomorrow," said Father. "I have to work."

"How about you, Mother?" asked the seven little mice.

"Not me!" said Mother. "I loved to ice fish when I was little. But now I'm afraid of slipping on the ice."

"Did Mother really go ice fishing when she was little?"
asked the seven little mice.

"Absolutely!" said Father. "She was a very fine fisherman.
We called her the Ice-Fishing Princess."

The seven little mice thought about that. How could they get Mother to go fishing with them? Suddenly they had an idea. They drew up a plan. Then they got to work cutting and hammering and tying.

"What on earth are you up to?" asked Mother.

"We can't tell you!" said the seven little mice. "It's a secret!"

The next morning, Mother was very surprised to see what they had made.

"Climb into the sled-chair!" cried the seven little mice. "We will push the Ice-Fishing Princess over the ice!"

Then they loaded some firewood onto the sled and left for the lake.

The seven little mice and Mother came to
the hole the weasels had made yesterday.

"Let's take turns!" said one little mouse.

"Me first!" said another.

"We'll switch as soon as you catch a fish!"
said a third.

"Here comes a fish! I caught it! I caught a fish!"

"Now you've got it!" said Mother. "When you've each caught a fish, we'll roast all of them for lunch."

Mother made a fire, but no more fish came.

"The first fish came so easily," said one little mouse. "But then what happened?"

"The fish must have gone somewhere else."

"I'm going skating."

The fire was ready, but there was still only one fish.
"The weasels caught so many yesterday." "Where have
the fish gone?" "Are they sleeping?" "I'm hungry!"

"It's your turn now, Ice-Fishing Princess," said the seven little mice. "Please catch us some fish! We need seven more—one for each of us."

So Mother took the fishing pole and dropped the line through the hole.

UMPH! There was a big tug on the line.

"A fish!" "It must be a big one!" "Pull hard, Mother!"

WHOOSH! The line came flying out of the hole—with eight fish on it.

"Wow!" "You did it!" "You caught eight fish at once!" "You really *are* the Ice-Fishing Princess!"

So seven little mice roasted eight fine fish right there in the middle of the frozen lake.

All seven little mice agreed—fresh-caught fish cooked over a fire was delicious!

"We have one fish left over," said Mother. "Who will we give it to?"

"FATHER!" said the seven little mice all together. And they took the ninth fine fish home to Father.